Windy Days

Heather Hammonds

Contents

The Wind

On some days, the wind blows.

Sometimes, there is very little wind.
Sometimes, it blows very hard.

The wind blows in trees and down streets.
It blows over the land and sea.

We can hear the wind blow,
on windy days.
We can feel the wind blow, too.
We cannot see the wind.

Hot and Cold Days

On hot, sunny days, the wind is warm.

People feel hot
when the warm wind blows.
It is very dry outside.

Sometimes, the wind is very cold.

People put on warm clothes.

They stay inside, out of the wind.

The Wind at Home

Some people put washing outside
on windy days.

The wind blows on the clothes.
The clothes dry quickly, in the wind.

Wind chimes are put outside,
in the garden.

Some wind chimes have bells.
The bells ring when the wind blows.

Plants and the Wind

Leaves blow from trees
on windy days.

In **autumn**, leaves fall from trees.

The wind blows hard.
It blows the leaves everywhere!

The wind blows seeds from some plants.
The seeds grow
when they fall to the ground.

The wind blows grass and flowers around, too.

The Wind and the Sky

On some days, there are **clouds** in the sky.
The wind blows the clouds.

Clouds move quickly across the sky
on windy days.

Birds fly around on windy days.

The wind helps some birds
fly high up in the air.

The Wind and the Sea

Some boats go very fast over the water on windy days.

The wind pushes the boats along.

The wind helps make lots of waves
on some days.

It is not safe for little boats
to go on the water
on very windy days.

Playing in the Wind

Some people play with **kites** on windy days.

The wind blows their kites up into the air.

People play with other toys
on windy days, too.

We can hear and feel the wind
when we are outside.

Glossary

autumn the season after summer

clouds tiny drops of water that float together in the sky

kites toys that can fly in the wind

wind chimes chimes that make sounds in the wind